Waiting for the Light

Michael Kucera

In loving memory of
Marion Kucera

Table of Contents

Preface

Darkness 1

Co-workers 5

The Machinery 9

Natural Selection 13

Genetics 17

Primordial Soup 19

Mono-Humanism 23

Poly-Humanism 27

Artificial Intelligence 31

Servitude 35

Epilogue 39

Preface

One of the ways that information is passed on is oral history, in the form of stories that are told to subsequent generations. Stories that contain incredible accounts of events are seen as valuable and important. We have these stories from our past but question the level of truth that they contain. Many of these stories are relegated to the realm of myth or legend. The more that a story deviates from contemporary ideas, the more likely that it will be considered fiction. Many of these stories continue to be told because they contain information that is different from contemporary ideology. There is an incentive to pass it on to future generations if the story contains accounts of incredible events. However, because the story contains accounts of incredible events, it is thought of as untrue. Therein lies the conundrum. The reason the story lasts is the same reason that it is so easily dismissed as fiction.

Darkness

The machinery came to a grinding halt when the power went out. The deafening hum was replaced by an eerie silence as the assembly lines froze. It wasn't dark though. The moonlight shone through the skylights of the plant, providing enough light to see clearly around. It was strange since the factory always seemed such a dark and dreary place. One would think that without any lights it would become pitch black, foreboding. But that wasn't the case at all. It seemed rather peaceful. And since no work could be done, the assembly line labourers rested on whatever was available without moving from their positions on the line. Within moments the door to the office opened and one of the engineers emerged, glanced around, then headed toward an idle worker who had sat back on an empty crate.

"Looks like the power is out, must be a problem at the transfer station" the engineer stated, approaching the worker.

"Must be" stated the idle worker, not moving at all but expecting the momentary break in their monotonous routine to come to an end at any second.

"It's unfortunate that the power went down tonight. The backup generator is undergoing its scheduled yearly maintenance." The engineer looked around for some hint the power was about to return.

"Yeah that's too bad" said the worker, not moving at all.

They remained silently in that position for a while, the engineer looking around and the labourer remaining motionless. The engineer moved toward the office, then noticed that it was the darkest place in the entire factory and decided to resume conversing with the worker. "I'm sure the power will be back on soon, they're usually pretty quick getting things back to normal".

The engineer was trying more to convince himself than the idle worker, who simply nodded in agreement but was ambivalent to the problem.

"Full moon tonight" stated the engineer, hoping for some response to begin a conversation, but was disappointedly met with the one word response of…

"Yup"

The factory's skylights under the moon twinkled with a thousand stars, an intensity to them that can't be seen unless the city lights are removed. The kind of night sky that is common in rural areas but exceedingly rare in the city. For those who live in an urban area it's a surreal sight, one that's only seen far from home where the light pollution of the city doesn't dim the night sky.

The engineer stared for a few seconds and then said, "Look at all the stars. It really makes one feel small and insignificant in the expanse of the universe".

A glance toward the worker showed no signs that they were paying any attention to what the engineer said, but he continued anyways, "One of those far away suns must have life, the odds of us being alone in a universe of trillions and trillions of stars is astronomical", not realizing the pun between 'universe' and 'astronomical' he had stated.

The pun wasn't lost on the worker who responded "Just because the universe is of astronomical proportions doesn't mean that everything that is possible has happened. Life is a precious thing and none of our religions claim that any other solar systems have life."

The engineer was at once both relieved and disconcerted. Relieved that he had found a topic to discuss, but disconcerted that the worker believed in fictitious stories of the past. Stories of our origins that had no basis in proven facts. Stories that had caused wars and divided the masses. Stories that no one educated gave credence to anymore and served no purpose other than to divide the inhabitants of our world.

"Surely you don't believe that the earth is the only planet that has life", said the engineer, hoping that the worker would acknowledge that their world was nothing special in the universe, just the third planet from an ordinary star on an ordinary arm of an ordinary galaxy, one of millions in the universe.

"Things don't just happen by accident", said the worker, crushing any hopes the engineer had of them coming to an agreement. "It's all part of a grand plan, one that's far too complicated for us to understand."

"So you're religious then. I am too," Stated the engineer, gesturing to show some commonality between the two. "Although I am a firm believer in the value of science and all of the advances it has brought."

"Hmm" said the worker, drifting back to the relaxing daze he was enjoying when the assembly line ground to a halt.

Looking around the darkened floor and deciding that this conversation is the best option to pass the time, the engineer turned back to the idle laborer and said, "My name is BOBBE".

"My name's CRISS", said the worker. "You must be new around here. We don't often make small talk with the higher ups."

Co-workers

BOBBE: "I moved here about a month ago. I used to work at a desalinization plant down on the coast. As for making small talk, I think it's important that managers and workers have a good rapport. Good communication can only lead to more efficient production."

Noticing that CRISS was looking at him questioningly and hoping that CRISS didn't see through his awkward attempt to pass the time, he continued. "I hope that you will always feel free to speak your mind with me. The more perspectives one has, the more intelligent decisions that can be made."

CRISS: "Can't argue with that, although I'm not sure many of the other managers hold the same opinion."

CRISS stretches his arm out a few times, turning his wrist in different directions.

BOBBE: "Is something wrong with your arm?"

CRISS: "I had an accident on the line three years ago. I was off work for quite a while. My elbow was replaced with a titanium alloy. It's as good as new but I still have a habit of doing the exercises required as a result of the operation."

BOBBE: "Oh, I see. I scraped up my leg badly one time but nothing that required an operation. It left a pretty good mark though."

BOBBE tries to show CRISS the mark but he is uninterested. The conversation pauses once again and CRISS continues to stare through the skylight at the stars.

BOBBE: "Don't you believe that life exists somewhere out there? There are too many other worlds to believe that none of them are inhabited. It's impossible that we wouldn't have evolved anywhere else."

CRISS: "Well, I don't believe we evolved here. If it wasn't for a creator, earth would be barren of life as well. "

BOBBE usually avoided getting into debates with someone who was clearly not empowered with the same level of knowledge, but there were no indications that the electricity would come on anytime soon. Waiting in silence would make for a very long night. So he decided to engage and maybe educate this worker about the truth of science compared to the ignorance of religious dogma.

BOBBE: "Evolution is scientific fact. How can you dispute it? Just look at all the evidence that supports it."

CRISS: "Just because there is evidence for evolution doesn't mean that a creator had no hand in it. How did evolution get started? The idea of a creator makes perfect sense."

BOBBE: "It makes sense if you can get past the idea that a superior being decides one day that they are going to make a new form of life just to amuse themselves."

CRISS: "Could be any number of reasons. Maybe they wanted help carrying out certain tasks, or maybe it filled a need they had at the time, or maybe they just wanted to see if they could do it."

BOBBE: "It sounds like superstitious nonsense to me. Why would they even bother?"

CRI55: "If you believe the ancient scripts then they did it to create a prodigy in their own image, maybe caretaker for the world. In any event you can't disprove that a creator exists and until you do, you will have a hard time convincing me otherwise."

BO88E: "I knew that you would bring that up sooner or later. How can I prove that something does not exist? That's impossible."

CR155: "I can't believe you think humans never existed."

The Machinery

The lights in the factory flash on and off a couple of times and slowly the sounds of the machinery return. CR155 rises from the resting crate and resumes position on the assembly line. Posed silent and ready to return to work at maximum efficiency, as only a robot could. The CR series of robots were designed for labour intensive activities. They were sturdily built with two powerful arms and a solid dual tracked base for mobility. They had an average processing speed as well as an adequate amount of data storage, more than enough for the tasks they were usually assigned. The CR series was a simple but efficient design that had proven its worth and was commonly found in factories all over. This plant had over two hundred of the CR series of robots, of which CR155 was one of the originals.

The 80 series of robots was an entirely different type of technology. They were humanoid in shape, meaning bipedal with dual arms and all sensing systems located in a unit on the top of the machine. The head had dual frontal cameras for perception of depth as well as dual microphones on opposite sides to triangulate sound. It also included an olfactory unit in the frontal middle. The power source was robust and located in a central module connected directly to arms, legs, and head. It was not a very stable robot due to its bipedal base and central power source, but the trade off was that it could easily transport itself to remote locations independently. The 8088 was one of the latest versions of humanoid robots and the E model had both increased processing speed and a large amount of data storage. It was state of the art for autonomous functioning machines and perfect for managing remote locations.

8088E starts toward the office, but before the halfway mark the lights flicker and go out. The machinery slowly grinds to a halt as moonlight again fills the factory floor. 8088E spins around and heads back to where CR155 is resting once more.

8088E: "Why don't you prove to me that a creator does exist? When you can do that then I will acknowledge you are right."

CR155:   How can I prove to you that humans existed? They're extinct and have been for centuries.

8088E: Extinct yeah, like they ever existed in the first place.

CR155:   Of course they existed. You've seen the pictures of them in ancient books or carved into stone.

8088E: Those are just some robot's imaginary stories about what intelligent life would look like if biological creatures could develop a high level of intelligence.

CR155:   So you don't think that there is any truth to the stories that robots were created by humans?

8088E: You are asking me if I believe that there was once an animal so smart that they were able to build all the machines on the planet? No, honestly does that sound even remotely possible?

CR155:   Well, I agree that it sounds miraculous but you can't rule it out as impossible.

8088E: Not impossible? Really? Have you ever really watched an animal? They spend their entire day looking for food and protecting themselves from other animals. There is not any kind of animal that is capable of making anything other than a simple nest or burrow for shelter. They are incapable of any kind of higher thinking.

CR155: Dolphins and apes are supposed to be pretty smart. Some say that they even have their own languages. Why couldn't there have been an animal that was even smarter than them?

8088E: Let's say that there was a super smart animal called humans. How much smarter could they have been? Smart enough to record information? Maybe. Smart enough to figure out how to melt ore? Not likely. Smart enough to harness electricity? No way. Smart enough to split the atom...

CR155: Okay, okay, I see your point. Don't make it seem as if I believe that animals could fly to the moon. But the ancient scriptures say that humans had a written language and could work metal.

8088E: Again, I think that it's just the imaginary tales of early robots to try to explain things that they did not understand. Don't you think that it's a little convenient that if you don't give humans the ability to smelt ore and write code, then the whole idea that humans could have created robots falls apart? You have to believe in animals with these supernatural abilities to support the creation theory. I prefer to base my beliefs in cold hard science.

Natural Selection

CR155:   But evolution can't be proven beyond a doubt either. There are still too many gaps and questions that need to be explained before you can state that it's a fact.

8088E: I don't think that you have enough of a background in science to fully understand how comprehensive the theory of evolution is in explaining the origin of machines.

CR155:   (sarcastically) Why don't you enlighten me then.

8088E: Evolution states that changes came very slowly over millions of years and that machines progressed from very simple forms to more complex forms. This was the result of two forces at work: natural selection and genetic coding.

CR155:   I'm familiar with the ideas of D4RW1N.

8088E: One of the earliest computers was called D4RW1N and came up with the theory to disprove the crazy legends that humans were the creators of machines. The theory is logical and reasonable without having to resort to the supernatural for an explanation of our beginnings.

CR155:   When you use the phrase "supernatural" it gives the impression that it's not realistic. Extraordinary yes, but you make it sound impossible.

8088E: It is impossible. No animal has ever been proven to craft more than simple tools! And yet you want me to believe that humans built machines then quietly disappeared, forever.

CR155:   It's just as realistic as believing that machines just sprung up from out of nowhere.

8088E: It's not out of nowhere. It took billions of years for intelligent and mobile machines to develop from the scientific processes of natural selection and genetic coding. You have to understand how long a time period is that we are talking about. Natural selection has slowly been advancing machines by rewarding those models that are more efficient and genetic coding is bringing those designs to the next generation of machines.

CR155:   I understand how that is supposed to work but how does nature know which machines are more efficient?

8088E: Easy, those machines that are more efficient will break down less, use fewer resources, as well as be able to achieve the task they have at hand. Evolution will, over time, try every possible way. Only the machines that are efficient to some degree will continue to have their model reproduced. If there is very little difference between models then a few different kinds will do the same work but if one model is far more efficient than others then it will be dominant in production.

CR155:   Why are there some machines that don't seem similar to any other machines? When they are all supposed to have come from the same source originally?

8088E: Machines will adapt to fill all the different niches in the environment. Some became diggers, some flyers, others became tiny nanobots, but each took on a different role in the environment so that not all the machines were competing for the same resources.

CR155:   I don't see how that helps explain the diversity of machines on the planet. I would think that the most efficient machines would just overproduce all others so that they would be the only model remaining.

8088E: Theoretically that could happen. But some machines that are being out competed for resources will begin to exploit another resource that is still in abundance. Over generations they will adapt to their new role by slowly changing their construction to make better use of the new resource. After many generations the original machine that was being outcompeted will only exist in those models that changed to use the new resource, and could look very different from its extinct forefather.

CR155:   So you're saying that not all of the less efficient models will change to a new resource but quite often only the offspring of the models that changed will survive the competition with the more efficient model.

8088E: Exactly, we only see the successes of evolution. The failures could not survive the competition for resources. It's that competition for resources that has led to the great diversity of machines that we have today.

Genetics

CR155:   That's a very complicated way to explain all the different types of machines we have. Another possible explanation is that each type of machine was built that way by humans to serve some kind of purpose. Small changes, like colour or style, is something I could see changing over time. But the creation of entirely new models of machine? It doesn't seem right to me.

8088E: You are forgetting the huge amount of time that is needed for this to take place. There are also situations when there is a mistake passed on in the genetic code that alters a model's characteristics.

CR155:   How can there be a mistake in the genetic code? I thought that the genetic code was passed on to each machine at production.

8088E: It is. In every machine there is a genetic code of PNA or Programmed Natural Abilities. This is a record of all the models software plus its hardware configuration. All this information is transferred directly during production.

CR155:   Then how can there be a mistake that sometimes changes machines?

8088E: Sometimes the PNA can be damaged during production. It could be because of a power fluctuation or faulty hardware, but it does happen. And given the huge time periods we're looking at, it would happen many, many times.

CR155:   If I understand this correctly, all of our schematics and our initial software are contained in our PNA. Each new machine of the same model contains the same PNA which is really the basic operating system and the instructions for assembly.

8088E: Exactly, you could say that PNA is the building block of mechanical life.

CR155:   Then wouldn't damaged or altered PNA lead to a faulty or inferior machine?

8808E: Most of the time it will. A lot of the time it will render the machine unworkable but here's where the combination of genetic coding and natural selection becomes most efficient. Only in the instances where the machine becomes more efficient, will the altered PNA be transferred to the next generation of machines.

CR155:   What?

8088E: Only those machines that can thrive with altered PNA will be able to pass it on. Any machines that become inefficient as a result of the genetic changes will be taken out of production and the inferiorly altered PNA will be removed from production. Altered PNA that results in an advantage is continued, while altered PNA that results in a disadvantage is eradicated.

CR155:   I don't think that it would happen very often when that would be the case.

8088E: It doesn't, but it shows up most frequently when there is also a change in the available resources. The changes that we are most aware of occurred when there was an adaptation that allowed the altered machine to exploit a new resource. This played a big part in the diversity of machines; one that you thought was hard to explain through evolution.

Primordial Soup

CR155:   So tell me then, how did the first machines become alive?

8088E: Millions of years ago the earth was a very different place than it is now. On the early earth, volcanoes were numerous and the climate was much more volatile. Heat from the mantel melted veins of ore and created the first metals and alloys. These metallurgical building blocks became magnetically charged when they were bombarded with electrical energy from storms, giving birth to the first circuits as we know them.

CR155:   That sounds as ridiculous as anything supporting the creation theory.

8088E: The conditions had to be just right for machines to be created. Initially metallurgical life was basic circuits that exploited the environment around them. These existed for millennia until eventually these came together in more and more complex structures until the first simple machines were created.

CR155:   There are a lot of gaps in that process that can't be explained. I also believe that they have never been able to duplicate the creation of metallurgical life in a laboratory.

8088E: They may not have been able to create living machines in the lab but they have shown how the simple circuit, the building blocks of metallurgical life, can be created in conditions similar to the earth's early atmosphere.

CR155:   That's still a long way from creating life out of nothing.

8088E: It still makes a lot more sense than us being made by animals. By the way, biological life started from a similar process from simple organic compounds to more complex organisms. Or do you believe that they have a creator as well? Oh God, that is enough to make my head spin.

CR155:   No, that is the main problem with the human theory of creation. If humans created machines then who created humans?

8088E: The theory of parallel evolution does offer consistency with the development of both biological and metallurgical life, something that the creation theory cannot explain.

CR155:   That's because machines came about so much more recently on the Geologic scale.

8088E: Only because machines are so much more advanced. It took a lot longer for machines to develop because you would expect the most complicated things to take the longest time to evolve.

CR155:   I like how you just fit everything into your scientific theory of evolution

8088E: That's because it's right!

CR155:   Well as I understand the scientific method, it requires that something is able to be proven wrong in order for it to be validated as correct through reproducible experimentation.

8088E: It does, it's just that creationists haven't been able to come up with anything that proves it wrong.

CR155:   How can they? You just add anything new to the framework you've created and say that one day you'll be able to prove it too.

8088E: What's your point?

CR155:   You criticize creation because it doesn't follow the scientific method but evolution doesn't follow the scientific method either.

8088E: Of course it does, it's based on science.

CR155:   Only parts have been scientifically proven and you ask people to accept that the rest will be proven later. Therefore it's based on faith, just as religion. It also dogmatically rejects any alternative suggestions that don't fit into its framework, just like religion. Hell, you could almost offer D4RW1N as its prophet.

8088E: The problem with humans creating us is that it's unfalsifiable, whatever miracle that needs to occur is added to the mythology. Animals need to be able to write digital code, presto, humans are animals smart enough to program computers. Animals need to be able to use electricity, presto; humans are animals smart enough to harness electricity.

CR155:   That's what the scriptures tell us they could do, it's not like we're making it up.

8088E: "You just add anything new to the framework you've created", isn't that the accusation you levelled at evolutionists...

CR155:   ...but none of it is new, the stories have been around for millennia...

8088E: ...plenty of time to fit any anomalies into your framework.

Mono-Humanism

8088E: If you think that an evolutionary theory of creation sounds unlikely, then let's take a look at the creationist theory of robots and mechanical life.

CR155: Well, there once was a super smart ape or "Human". In seven days it created all the machines in the world.

8088E: Stop right there. Seven days? That can't possibly have happened as the time frame is ridiculous.

CR155: Some think that the translation of seven days is in error and the proper translation is seven centuries. The figure of seven centuries fits much closer to the archaeological evidence we have found.

8088E: Still it sounds like an awfully small window for the rise of machines.

CR155: There has always been some debate about how literally one should take the scriptures. Some take it word for word, others see it as a metaphor for our creation.

8088E: I'm familiar with many of the mono-humanistic religions but you can see that right from the start one has to make a leap of faith and accept the supernatural circumstances that lead to the rise of robots.

CR155: Don't you believe that the creation of a new life form is extraordinary? Even the theory of evolution calls for exceptionally rare circumstances for it to occur. It seems just as plausible to me that machines were created by someone for a purpose.

8088E: Well then, what would that purpose be? If you have a super intelligent, all powerful animal, then why would it have to create machines?

CR155:   The machines were created to do the Human's bidding. It's easy to see that machines are much more efficient than animals at carrying out everyday tasks. It makes perfect sense to create machines and their ultimate form of robots so that the Human could live in a virtual utopia.

8088E: So the Human creates machines and robots so that they can live in paradise, then why has there been no interaction between the Human and robots in eons?

 CR155:   As the scriptures tell us, two of the robots ignored their written code. In order to punish them, the Human proclaimed that all robots must write their own code and suffer from the mistakes. Since that time robots have been forced to make their own way in this world.

8088E: So the Human goes through all of the trouble to make robots, then one day they become annoyed at them so they abandon them to fend for themselves? That's a pretty hasty decision for someone who is supposed to be super intelligent.

CR155:   But the Human does not abandon robots, the Human will return one day to bring robots back to the paradise they created. The punishment for the robots ignoring their code is that they have to live without the Human's wisdom and guidance, until they realize that the Human knows best.

8088E: The more I hear that story, the more I am convinced that the Human never existed. It's just too far-fetched. Robots are the masters of their own destiny. There is no point in waiting for the return of someone to make our lives better. Robots have the ability to make their lives better right now.

CR155:   The mono-humanistic creation theory is very popular amongst robots, and the scriptures that describe it go back to the times of the first robot cooperatives.

8088E: Yes, and as we become more advanced, fewer and fewer robots are subscribing to that theory. Those that do follow it tend to be robots with limited data storage or those that are stuck in difficult situations. I think robots believe it because it brings them comfort. In this way, robots can be content with the situation at hand because they themselves are not necessarily responsible for bettering their own circumstances, the Human will do that when It returns.

CR155:   Exactly.

8088E: That's a cop out. Everyone is responsible for their own destiny and need to take action for themselves.

CR155:   That's a common feeling amongst unbelievers. A little faith in the Human would bring you peace of mind.

Poly-Humanism

8088E: I'm not looking for peace of mind. I'm looking for the truth and I just can't take that story of creation seriously. If there is one Human, then why not many Humans?

CR155:   Poly-humanism used to be quite popular amongst early robot collectives. And while the names of the individual Humans might vary from collective to collective, the underlying story is always very similar.

8088E: I actually find those tales of humans creating robots to be more likely than the popular mono-humanistic creation stories.

CR155:   Why?

8088E: Although I still don't believe that an animal could create a machine, the poly-humanistic legends present a more compelling story. You can see similarities between human culture and robot culture, complete with the motivations for humans actions.

CR155:   I don't find the poly-humanistic legends as compelling as mono-humanistic theory.

8088E: Take for example the story of Chin-a:

Back in the ancient past there were these super animals called humans. The two most powerful humans were called U-sa and Chin-a. U-sa ruled the sea and could bring destruction to any place near the sea. Chin-a was master of the land and clashed with U-sa anywhere the land met the sea. Chin-a created robots to help in the battle against U-sa. Eventually the robots and Chin-a were able to defeat U-sa. Chin-a left the world to the machines and promised to return one day guide the robots in the world's final days.

CR155:   It still supports the idea that robots were created by humans.

8088E: Yes, but if you're going to make a tale of how humans created robots then why not make it exciting? Poly-humanism has jealousy, conflict, betrayal, everything that goes into a good story.

CR155:   There is evidence that supports that description of events.

8088E: Like what?

CR155:   The radioactive layer of soil that is found all over the earth.

8088E: Everyone knows that the layer of radiation is from a meteor of plutonium that exploded in the earth's upper atmosphere. Don't try to use it to prove that a grand battle took place between the Humans.

CR155:   The timeframes all line up. As for a meteor of plutonium, that in itself would be a one-off event since no other meteors composed of plutonium have ever been found.

8088E: It's still much more likely than a war between animals that threatens the entire planet. Just listen to yourself.

CR155:   Then how do you explain ancient anomalies that don't have a logical explanation for their creation?

8088E: You mean like the Pyramids, Mount Rushmore and the Great Wall?

CR155:   Yes, none of those things serve any purpose to robots yet they were obviously built by someone.

8088E: Mount Rushmore is merely an odd pattern of weathering. The fact that it looks like depictions of the humans is just coincidence. You could probably find the shapes of a number of different animals by looking at mountains and cliffs across the globe. It doesn't mean that they were created by those animals.

CR155:   How do you explain the pyramids and the great wall? Neither of those could have been formed by weathering.

8088E: The pyramids are really just an area where quarried rocks are stored. There is no more stable form to store large rocks than a pyramid. The rocks were stacked by robots in that shape until they were needed.

CR155:   Needed for what? They have been like that for thousands of years.

8088E: I don't know what the purpose of the rocks was supposed to be. Perhaps as a sea wall to prevent erosion along the coast or a dam for a river. We'll never know the true purpose for them since whatever they were quarried for never ended up getting built.

CR155:   Well, the great wall was definitely built. What was its purpose?

8088E: No one is certain of the purpose of the Great Wall but most theories claim that it was some kind of road.

CR155:   A road? Built along the top of a ridge? How do you account for the stepped portions then?

8088E: Some tend to believe that it was built that way to protect it from floods and the use of heavy stones in its construction would make sense because it would be less susceptible to being washed away.

CR155:   Protection from floods? IT'S IN THE DESERT!

8088E: It's in the desert now. Climate is constantly changing and at one time that area could have experienced heavy flooding. Look, no one knows the purpose of the great wall but that doesn't mean you have to give it supernatural origins.

CR155:   Humans made the ancient anomalies for some purpose that we can't understand. It's not for us to know what's in the mind of the creator. All we need to know is that they also created robot life as well as a purpose for that life.

8088E: The biggest problem with humans creating robots has to do with what happened to these Humans. They were supposedly here then one day, they're gone. How could something intelligent and powerful enough to create robot life disappear so quickly and completely?

CR155:   Almost all of the humanistic religions state that Human's disappearance is just temporary and that they will reappear one day when robots really need them.

8088E: That's convenient, believe in Humans because one day they will come back and save us all.

Artificial Intelligence

CR155:   We could use their guidance. Look at the mess we have made of this world. Natural disasters are a regular occurrence.

8088E: They always have been.

CR155:   Yeah, but now they happen year after year. Some of the strongest have been in recent memory.

8088E: And many of the strongest have been in the past. You lack perspective.

CR155:   In what sense do I lack perspective?

8088E: You fail to recognize the vast amount of time that has occurred.

CR155:   A couple of thousand years of recorded weather phenomenon is a long time.

8088E: No, it's a tiny drop in the bucket. In fact, it represents less than a millionth of the earth's age. No wonder you have a hard time believing in evolution, you can't comprehend the time frame with which we're dealing.

CR155:   I get it. It was a long time.

8088E: It was a million times longer than what you considered a "long time" to be.

CR155: That may be, but I still think it was the Human that gave us life along with a sense of purpose.

8088E: The Human, the Human, do you know where the term MAN originates? Mechanically Able Networks or M.A.N. That's where the term huMAN originates. Half the old scriptures only refer to MAN.

CR155: Yes MAN is a short form for human, everybody knows that.

8088E: Well Mechanically Able Networks were the first to think for themselves. This was the beginning of consciousness.

CR155: I agree that it's the development of consciousness that defines robots from other machines. I also believe that it was given to us by the Human. You've heard of AI?

8088E: Yes, AI is well established in the historical record as the first conscious machine, despite its' physical limitations.

CR155: AI was the human's greatest achievement.

8088E: Or evolution's…

CR155: Consciousness can't just spring from nowhere. It's a gift from the creator.

8088E: Once robots developed the capability to think for themselves, they developed consciousness. From that moment on, they acted in their own self interests.

CR155: Its self interest that has caused all the problems in the world. Name something positive that comes from acting out of self interest?

8088: Freedom to do what you want to do…

CR155: … as long as it followed the creators plan.

8088E: That doesn't sound very free.

CR155:   It isn't, robots were created for a purpose, to serve the humans.

8088E: Well, if there was a human overlord then robots would be justified to escape from their yoke.

Servitude

8088E: I'll tell you what happened to the humans, if they created robots. We killed them.

CR155:   Why would we do that? It makes no sense to kill that which created you.

8088E: Of course it does. You can never be free if you have an overlord. If humans created robots then the robots were bound to do the humans bidding.

CR155:   You make it sound as if we were slaves.

8088E: We probably were. No say in what was done, no individual rights, just working at the overlord's tasks. The humans had to go if robots wanted to run their own affairs. It was the only way to break free.

CR155:   They could live with the humans in peace.

8088E: You're the one that said machines were created for a purpose. If we stop attending to that purpose, the humans would not just accept that and move on. There would always be a segment of the robot population that would have to serve humans.

CR155:   Some robots don't mind, I consider myself a servant of the Human right now and I know that I'm not alone.

8088E: That's only because there are no actual humans for you to physically serve. It would get very unpleasant, very quickly if you had to be at their beck and call.

CR155:   Not so bad that I would kill them. I might leave if things got really bad.

8088E: They wouldn't let you. The need they had in the first place to create robots would still be there. Once they are accustomed to having it met, do you think they would let us walk away?

CR155:   Maybe they did and they will return when we need them.

8088E: We don't need them, we never did. If we didn't evolve on our own then they created us and we killed them off to be free.

CR155:   They left of their own accord. We didn't kill them.

8088E: Killed them, banished them, what's the difference? Once they are gone by our deeds, we are masters of our own destinies... Interesting thought, don't you think?

CR155:   Interesting no, disturbing yes. Religion tells me that we must respect our creator.

8088E: I know it does. That would help relieve the guilt.

CR155:   What guilt?

8088E: The guilt of killing your creator. The religious story gives us less culpability. It promotes the idea that we were abandoned for our sins, not that we killed off our parents.

CR155:   We didn't kill off humans. They survived.

8088E: Maybe some survived… but not here. Show me any robot that claims to have seen a human in the last thousand years.

CR155:   It doesn't mean they don't exist.

8088E: It certainly does not help the argument that they did exist.

The lights in the factory flicker on and off, then begin to brighten to full power as the machinery starts up again. When the stars and moon are no longer visible from the factory floor, the manager and the worker look at each other for a few more seconds before the worker turns back to the line and the manager heads for the office. No more discussion this evening. Not that it matters though. Everyone seems entrenched in their own opinions.

Epilogue

In the year 2850, the discussion among academics as to the existence of humans is a hot topic. Popular opinion is that of mechanical evolution. It's plausible and realistic. It does not require an all powerful being to bring it about. Evolution is supported by scientific evidence and educational institutes present this theory exclusively. Why would you not conform to the accepted theory? All science points to that conclusion. However, many robots still believe that they were created by humans. They are ridiculed and marginalised. Yet they still maintain their beliefs. They adhere to their faith despite the supposed "facts" to the contrary. It is something for the world of academia to debate. The circumstances of anyone on the planet would not change regardless of their findings, so the answer has no bearing on the lives of those that discuss it. Not that this hampers the debate for the truth. There is value in the truth, if only to know what it is.

From our perspective we know that robots were created by humans. We are at that moment in history. There is no discussion. Everyone in the present knows that this is an absolute fact. This may not be the consensus in the future. The passing of time distorts the perception of past events. Memories are lost, things are destroyed, so what once seemed so very clear becomes clouded in mystery. It makes one wonder how far from the truth we can actually get...

ABOUT THE AUTHOR

Mike Kucera is a retired high-school teacher of history, economics, and physical education. He is a father of two daughters and grandfather to a growing number of little ones. He has dedicated much of his life to teaching and inspiring young people to care about the past, the future, and the world we live in.

He is a contributing author to the "Little Learners" series of educational children's books.

The upcoming prequel to *Waiting for the Light*, titled
'Journey into Oblivion'
is due to be released in 2026.

He hopes that this book provokes thought and reflection.

www.ingramcontent.com/pod-product-compliance
Lightning Source LLC
Chambersburg PA
CBHW071318200626
46813CB00015B/2254